Flipped

By
Yazmine Mobley

Thanks for your support
god bless you

Mayre ♡

A Young Urban Author Publication

Copyright 2012

Yazmine Mobley

Cover Design: Fusion Creative Works

Developmental Editor: Dr. Jeffrey Perkins Jr.

Publisher: Young Urban Authors

www.youngurbanauthors.org

ISBN-13:978-1481008044

ISBN-10:1481008048

Library of Congress Control Number (applied for)

Acknowledgements

I would like to thank the City of Seattle for funding the Seattle Youth Violence Prevention Initiative, without its funding the Young Urban Authors program would not have been possible. I also would like to thank Ms. Frankie Roe for pushing me to keep writing, and I want to thank my mother for motivating me by giving me deadlines that I had to meet. I also want to thank my dad for making sure I was in a quiet environment. Finally, I want to thank my peers and teachers for their motivation and I thank God for giving me the strength to finish writing my story.

Dedication

This book is dedicated to anybody and everybody that has found someone they love, and when separated by distance, knows how unbearable it can be.

CONTENTS

PART I

FLORIDA

"Sekeya Mae! Wake up, you have to take a shower! We have to go to the mall and finish shopping before four o'clock! Get up booger." I could hear my mom yelling from the kitchen and her footsteps approaching. I groan and roll off my bed on to the floor falling onto my left side. "Well that's going to leave a bruise," my mom said. "Just get up and stop acting so dramatic." She chuckled looking at me. "You can *spazz-out* on the plane sweetheart." I smiled and said in my most sarcastic tone, "you are such a loving mother Maria Jackson." Then she blew me a kiss and left my doorway. My body felt tensed as I eased myself up slowly off the unforgiving cold floor and lazily walked to the bathroom.

I undressed myself and took a shower. Once I finished I started getting dressed. I looked into the mirror while taking my pink bonnet off and I smoothed my sleek black hair back and pull my hair up into a "princess bun." I tried smoothing the edges of my hair under it but all my attempts to perfection simply failed, so I shrugged my shoulders, gave up, and thought I'll put on a headband and forget it—too bad!

Finally, we arrived at the airport and after three hours of anticipation and irritation checking in and all, at last I was able to take a seat on the plane in the last row. I hate sitting in front seats. Even though my parents were in front seats, my sister and I decided to play it safe by sitting in the back. That's because she's like me and doesn't like hearing our parents conversations. I start thinking to myself and begin to write about the kind of guy, I would like to date. I write why the perfect guy for me would have to have morals, be sensitive but not immature. Regarding LOVE? At least real love, he will have in his heart. He has to love me just like I love him, a 50/50 relationship, and he has to have family values. I'm thinking if a guy treats his mom like a princess, chances are he will treat you the same. Suddenly, my sister starts to shift on my shoulder as she tries to fall asleep. I let her rest as I continue to write in my journal about my personal *My-My* story. When I finished writing about my morning journey to get to the plane, I put my pink, white, black, and purple journal into my large paint splattered carry-on bag and I soon after fell asleep.

Once we get to the baggage claim area, another family was there claiming their bags, next to us: three women, two men, four girls and three boys. They varied in color from light to dark skinned.. When I saw my bag coming onto the carriage cart, I reached to grab it, and at the same time, a light skinned boy grabbed it first. Our hands met for about three warm seconds and when I looked at him, he smiled back at me. That's when I pulled my hand away and he lifted my bag onto our caravan. In a small but nice conversation, we exchanged Facebook names and went our separate ways. His name was My'Trell Foxx.

We arrived at the airport at about 11:00 o'clock p.m., Florida time and it was hot. Nonetheless, I was wide awake from my encounter meeting with *My'trell Foxx*, and he's so cute. My dad rents a really nice rental car, a sports car of some sort. Also, that's when my sister and I tell our parents we're hungry, and they take us to a waffle house to get some food for dinner. Our hotel was only a few blocks away. So, I patiently wait to get into our room. It was a big room with a clear view to a blue pool outside, and we had a kitchen where I set down to eat. When I finished I took another shower and changed into pajamas. Soon after my shower, I watched the news and crawled into bed and fell asleep.

The next morning we woke up at about 10:00 o'clock. I woke up quietly and went to brush my teeth, wash my face, take a shower after my little sister, and finally I got dressed. I put on a pair of light *daisy dukes,* a style of shorts, a white and pink Hollister shirt, and a pair of pink and white gladiator sandals.

We drove to the port, showed our passes, and boarded a huge all-white Carnival cruise ship: The Fantasy. I remember walking down a long line that was forming with my purple suitcase in one hand, my paint splattered bag on one shoulder, and a bottle of ice water in a bag on the other. As I stepped into a large building I could see people throwing their bottled water away. I remember rolling my eyes and drinking the rest of mine in a series of fast gulps. Suddenly, I heard someone chuckling. I recalled it was a chuckle to a familiar face. I turn around and saw him doing the same, gulping of the water from a water bottle he had in his hand. When he finished he stated, "I'm not wasting my water either." My eyes bulged at him and I said, *"My'trell?"* He smiled and said, "hey Sekeya." That's when I laughed and said to him, "I swear you're stalking me!" He laughed and said, "you're funny…let's kick it…I mean you're gonna cruise for eight days, right?" I nod and only replied. "Mmm…." That's when my mom called me saying: "Come on Keke!" And I looked at *My'trell* and waved as I left him. He waved back and walked back to his brothers.

After we had registered and took some pictures, I went to my cabin. It had a nice view of the ocean water, it was so calming. I walked out into the hallway and sure enough *My'trell's* room was right across from mine. He

15

grins when he noticed me and said: "Keeps getting better huh?" I replied, "Kinda." He then suddenly hugs me tightly and whispered to me, "and better beautiful." I blushed and said, "Yes but it shouldn't be hun...I barely know you and your holding me as if I'm your girlfriend." That's when he let me go and his facial expression changed to disappointment. I shook my head and again said questioningly; *"My'trell?"* He looked at me with a face of embarrassment and replied, "Yes Sekeya." That's when I walked closer into his personal space and boy did he look surprised when my hand touched his neck, and I slowly stepped up onto my tippy-toes and kissed him on the cheek. Both his cheeks turned red as I whispered, "I never said it was a bad thing *My'trell* but I just barely know you." And when I proceeded to walk away, he grabbed me by the hand. And once again, I begin to think about that first night at the airport where we first met.

Then he kissed me on my cheek and I smiled. He said to me, "Meet me on the sky deck at 7:30 and dress up in something that you would wear to a party." "We got eight days, right?" I nodded my head, smiled and asked him, "a date and yes?" He smiled and replied, "it's gonna be much more than that."Then I laughed and said, "You aren't Trey Songz…fool!" He looked at me up and down with a strange look in his eyes. Our eyes met and he winked at me. "You say that now babe. Wait 'til later." I rolled my eyes and said "sure but I'll see you tonight…now I have to go get my nails done."

PART II

MY'TRELL

I get my nails painted with the color of white French tips and I get my toe nails with the same. I go back to my room and pull my hair into a bun and twist my bangs and clipped them back, and I slick down my baby hairs. Next, I put on eye liner, mascara and make blue smoky eyes. Then I put on a pair of white ripped jeans, a navy blue and white striped Hollister-belly top and a navy blue cardigan to match, and I put on a pair of navy blue toms that were the same color as my ring finger polish with a white and silver flower. The rest of my nails have French tips with a navy blue flower on each finger. Finally I get my navy blue coach wristlet and put in my lip balm, eyeliner, and mascara. I also put in my room key, ID, some sweet gum, $75, my phone, iPod, headphones, and a writing pad. It's around 7:15 p.m. when I'm finished getting ready. I walk outside and immediately see *My'trell* waiting for me leaning against his room door listening to his iPod and slowly bobbing his head. Startled I scream and he looked up at me and smiled. He took out one head phone and said, "Sorry ma, I didn't mean to scare you," and then he started chuckling. I rolled my eyes and crossed my arms in a childish motion and pouted. He hugged me and said, "Okay…I'm sorry for laughing at you baby girl…you forgive me?" I said to him, "no," in a baby voice and buried my face in his chest. He smelled really good, I thought and I inhaled deeply. And once again, he laughed.

"You're so strange, first you mad at me and now you're smelling me."

"I'm still mad at you," I mumbled, "no matter how good your smell." And then I proceeded to uncross my arms and wrap them around him instead.

"Then why are you hugging me?" he retorted and laughed.

"Fine, I won't hug you then." I tried to pull away but he hugged me tighter; smelling me, and I just shook my head and laughed.

20

"Never said I didn't want your hugs Sekeya," he said. Then he kissed my forehead.

"Never said I didn't want to go to the sky deck either, but you're holding me in the middle of the hallway on a ship somewhere random in the Atlantic Ocean."

Then he laughed and said: "Oh yeah, come on let's go."

He bent over to tie his shoe and I slapped his butt. He froze in motion for about ten seconds, and then finished tying his shoe.

"I hope you know I'm going to get you back for that," he mumbled.

"No you aren't." I started to run but he stood up and ran behind me catching me by the waist. He held me close to him and instantly it calmed me down.

"I feel like everything is strangely perfect." He mumbled. "Me too," I said. But he started rubbing my sides and said, "I like you. But you already knew that…huh?"

" Kinda," I said. "I think it was just luck that we ended up at the same airport and on the same cruise liner." I said in a delicate but sarcastic voice.

"I'm sure it was destiny babe. I would love to hold you here in the middle of the hallway on a ship somewhere, random in the Atlantic Ocean but we have plans baby girl so let's go." he said, and then he let me go.

I looked him up and down, and thought, 'He's really cute…he's light skinned with full lips, a square jaw, almond shaped eyes, long eye lashes, thick but contained eye brows, a thin mustache, peach fuzz on his chin, curly hair and no acne—I'm so jealous.' He was wearing a silver linked chain, two diamond studs, a white Hollister v-neck (to show off his muscles, I believe), distressed men's ripped sleeveless jacket (that was really cool looking), a pair of levis the same classic jean blue as the jacket with the bottoms cuffed, a silver spike belt to match his chain I assumed, a silver and diamond watch, and a pair of fresh air force ones with no creases.

He noticed me staring at him spacing out and kissed me on my lips. "Earth to baby girl?" he said, "you alright ma? Just in case…I just stole a kiss while you're spacing so you can't hit me, I'm trying to save you."

I laughed and blushed at the same time and I said: "I was admiring your swag hun, and you have to ask before you kiss me or I'm gonna hit you next time."

"Sorry," he said, "but your lips are soft."

"Whatever hun, let's go," I replied and started walking away. That's when he caught up with me and reached out and held my hand, then our fingers locked.

"I like your nails ma."

"Thank you… and by the way, you have soft lips too"

We walked to the central lobby of the ship and to the glass elevator. I tried to press the button but he said, "No" and I put my hand back at my side. He walked me to the regular elevators because I told him the glass one makes me nervous. He pressed the button and said, "It's my responsibility to make sure you feel like a princess tonight. So you don't have to lift a finger around me." I started to pout and I mumbled, "I'm a big girl," and folded my arms and pulled them to my chest forgetting he was holding my hand.

He laughed and said, "Yes I know, but at the moment though your boob is getting pretty acquainted with my hand."

I shook my head and said, "I'm such a ditz. I forget I have them sometimes"

"No you aren't baby girl," he said with a smile, "and don't trip, I'll remember for you." And then he put his hand back to his side.

'DING' goes the elevator door.

"C'mon babe" he said, still holding my hand. We stared into each others' eyes for what felt like forever. I can see by looking into his eyes that he's had a rough past, but he's focused on me now and he sincerely likes me. It feels like I've known him for forever. As I'm deep in thought he leaned closer to kiss me. This time I kissed

24

him back as he pressed me against the wall and our tongues collided. But as his hands started to explore me, the elevator seem to jerk to an abrupt stop, and I was kind of happy it did. I was not ready for that. We heard another DING, the elevator stopped, he smiled and said: "C'mon *shorty*, it's our stop."

The floor was dimly lit with red, yellow, purple, green, and orange lights hanging from the ceiling. The room was like a classy restaurant and smelled of fragrant and greatly seasoned food. I smiled and locked my fingers between his before I started walking. I tried to squeeze his hand but his hand was so much bigger than mine. "Damn you have big hands hun," I said. When he shook his head and mumbled, "Nah you're just really small so everything seems big to you…Leprechaun girl." I rolled my eyes at him and he stopped walking and stared at me for a second or two. I asked him what's wrong and I got no answer. He just calmly looked at me and exhaled. Then he grabbed me and hugged me loosely just to whisper in my ear, "I'm nervous. I actually have 'butterflies' and I've never had them before."

"Aye...you'll get over those butterflies," I said, "I'm easy to get used to."

"Are you sure?"

"Mmm humm….as sure as the waitress was about us being two crazy people"

"Oh damn, you're right. We should get a table,"

"Okay, let me go now."

"I don't want to."

"What did you make the reservation under?"

"My'trell" I laughed and wiggled out of his arms and walked over to the pale skinny waitress and said, "Do you have reservations for *My'trell?"*

"Yes right this way," she said.

I motioned for *My'trell* to follow me. The waitress put the menus down on a marble candle lit table. *My'trell* pulled my seat out for me and I set down smiling like an idiot. He set down and looked confused.

"Why are you smiling so much?" He said.

"Nobody's ever done that to me before?" I replied.

"What? I don't know what you're talking about."

"Nobody's ever pulled my seat out for me."

"Why not?"

"I don't know."

He stared at me for a second with a concerned look on his face. I looked away, I didn't want him to try and pry at my emotions. Instead, I started fondling with my menu, while he mumbled something under his breath that I couldn't quite hear.

"What did you say?" I asked,"Oh I was just saying that I'm paying for everything tonight"

"You don't have to... I said, "I have some money."

"I want to...you're my princess."

27

"Of all the girls on this ship, why do you want me to be your princess?"

"You just have something that's special about you."

"Like what?"

"You are…."

In the middle of his sentence the skinny pale waitress interrupted us. "Welcome to World Wide Voyage, what would you like to drink?"

"Raspberry lemonade," I replied.

The waitress was staring at *My'trell* the entire time I was giving her my order. *My'trell* didn't even seem to notice. He was playing with my finger nails. And now obviously annoyed, the waitress said to him: "And for you handsome?"

My'trell smiled, cleared his throat and said, "Same." And he still didn't look at her.

"Anything else for you," she said; then touched his neck while biting her lower lip.

He pulled away disgustingly and said: "That was inappropriate of you. You're a grown woman, I'm a child. And it was disrespectful since I'm obviously on a date with my girl."

"I'm sorry, don't start b*tchin," she said.

"May I please speak with your manager?"

"F#@k it…sure!" She snapped, and stormed away obviously upset. That's when he pulled my hands to his face and inhaled deeply. "No need to act like a b*@#$ because you're with a girl. All I did was touch you."

"Back to the sniffing," I said with a smile.

"Is it awkward? I mean…you really do smell good…like candy"

I remember laughing and just saying: "Thank you."

He kissed my hand and said: "Never a problem baby girl."

I smile and his expression changed to a seductive look. He divided my index and middle finger and slowly licks in between them. Than he winked at me right after he pulled his tongue back in his mouth.

I laughed and said, "No."

He started to pout and kiss all of my fingers slowly and I smiled and pulled my right hand out of his face and replaced it with the left one.

He licked between my index finger and middle finger again in the same fashion then he proceeded kissing all my fingers. That's when I giggled and put my hand on the table. Then for about thirty seconds, we gazed into each others' eyes. A plump white lady with red hair and hazel eyes came over to our table carrying our drinks. "Sorry for the inconvenience," she said. "What exactly did the waitress do?"

He looked at the woman and said, "Inappropriate misconduct. She touched my neck and when I told her how inappropriate it was, she got upset and cursed multiple times." "Oh, I'm sorry sir. I will be the waitress for you and your lovely lady tonight. Have you decided on what you want to order?"

"Yes, I would like the tour of Italy."

"Okay, and you ma'am?"

"I would like the same."

"Okay, please enjoy your free appetizer that's on the way, and sorry for the inconvenience."

"Thank you." We both said.

The waitress grabbed our menus and strolled to the other side of the large restaurant. It was strangely quiet, and there were only about eight other people. *My'trell* looked at me calmly, and I laughed and asked, "What's up?"

"Nothin' I never finished my explanation."

"About what?"

"Why you're the only girl that I wanted out of all the females on ship."

"Oh…okay…why?"

31

"You're sweet, funny, weird, silly, short, pretty, you seem smart, insightful, peaceful, responsible, swagger, caring, mature, modest, innocent…actually I take that back. You act innocent but I think you're low-key freaky."

I laughed and said to him: "Thank you and how am I not innocent? You're the one lickin' and kissin on my fingers."

He smiled and said, "I never said I was innocent, and I'm not gonna act like I am, baby girl."

"Whatever, Mr. McNasty"

"I like that name Mrs. McNasty"

"Mmm…whatever," I said.

Then he laughed. "Okay I'm just kidding Sekeya but on a serious note I really do like you."

"I like you too *My'Trell*"

"Good"

Our appetizer came, boneless hot wings. "Oh lord I love hot wings," I mumbled.

"Me too," he said.

I grab one and bit it. It was so tender till it fell apart in my mouth and the seasoning and sauce was amazing. Before I could bite it again, he took the rest of the wing out of my hand and ate it.

"You're on time out."

"Never, and that hot wing was on slap"

"Yeah I know, it was mine too."He laughed and said, "Maybe that's why it was so good. Besides what if they were nasty? I might as well bite yours instead of having to get my own."

"What kinda logic is that fool?" I asked.

"Mine." He said.

"DUH?" He grabbed another one, bit it, and hands the rest to me saying, "peace offering?"

"Only because you're a cutie," I said, smiled, and I ate the rest of the wings with him in silence.

Our food came soon afterward. It was lasagna, chicken parmesan, chicken linguini, a roll and a Caesar salad. We ate in silence exchanging looks here and there. I finished before him and finished my lemonade as well. He grinned while he ate the last of the lasagna. When he finished I was curious as to why he was still grinning. He started to reach for my hands and playfully pulled away, then he started laughing and said, "Why can't I touch your hands *speedy*?"

I laughed and asked him: "Why I gotta be speedy? I'm not fast you're just slow."

"I think the way you eat is cute." He replied.

"How is eating Italian food cute?"

"I'm Italian so you're basically eating my culture and I'm black so it's okay if you eat it. I mean you're not dark skinned but you're like…beige I guess."

"I'm Italian, Native American and Black. So we share two races, and you're just yellow like Winnie the Pooh."

"You think you're funny Sekeya Mae."

"Yes, I should have my own talk show."

"Uum…hum."

We both started to laugh and I reached across the table to touch his dimples.

He laughed and reached into his pocket to get his wallet. I retracted my hand to get my wallet and grab some money. Without looking at me he laughed and said, "Why are you trying to pay? I already told you that you were a princess tonight."

"I also can pay for myself tonight, and it's okay"

"I'm not allowing that."

"Fine… bossy."

He picked up the bill and put about $60 into it. Then he reached across the table and touched my hand, and we left the restaurant holding hands and walking calmly. As we approached the elevator I reached into my purse and grabbed a piece of gum, put it in my mouth, and offered *My'trell* one. He accepted it silently and I could tell that he was plotting something. That's when the elevator door opened to an empty elevator. We stepped inside, and I moved in the corner as he pressed the button for the highest point on the ship. I believe it was the 14th floor and we were only on the 3rd floor.

As soon as the door closed *My'trell* instantly was hugging me. He put his arms around me and we hugged for about five seconds. Then he bent down and gently kissed me, and I kissed him back. Our tongues collided and the gum came in handy. We kissed until we reach our floor.

DING! We walked out of the elevator and seem to be in the sky deck area. Besides the bartender at the mini bar by the elevator door, we were the only people up there

36

at 8:45p.m, and the humid tropical breeze really felt good on my skin.

The sunset was gone but the heat stayed. We sat down at a white table with candles, ate chocolate covered strawberries with whipped cream, and talked about his family history and his past. He talked fast and quietly with a sense of nervousness. He said "My mom is Black and my father is pure Italian. I have a few siblings but we're all spread out except for me and my sister My'leahsha who is two years younger than me. My parents are divorced, and my dad has a new wife. My mom met my stepdad and now they have all these damn kids and I have a brother and a sister. He's a *b*tch Nigga* though. He tries to act like I'm his kid. I'm basically like no f@*k you! But yeah, life's good. I'm 16, I live in Detroit, I like music...and yeah...what about you *shortie*?

"Well that sounds kinda rough, aren't people from rough lives supposed to be kinda mean?"

"Yeah, to be honest I am pretty rude, but I ain't gonna lie to you."

"You're not rude to me."

"That's because you're special to me."

"How?" I asked. "We just met."

"You're beautiful, funny, compassionate, silly, short, energetic, and bubbly, and you have a funny accent. You have a special glow about you, when you smile it pulls me in. I know I sound corny as f#@k but its Gucci baby girl."

I laughed for a while then blushed. "Thank you sweetheart," I said, but how do I have a funny accent? I just have a high voice. You're the one that sounds like Delano Edwards with your deep voice and baby face? Where they do that at?"He grinned at me, shook his head for a few seconds, and grabbed a strawberry and ate it with a smile. Then he said, "Now that you all up in my mind, tell me your story."

I pondered for a second and said, "Humm...well...I'm African American, Native American, Italian, and Japanese. I love music, pretty things, cute guys, strawberries, pineapples, peaches, pomegranate and star fruit. I also like veggies, rain, puppies and shopping. My parents are mood swingers. Sometimes they wanna kiss and cuddle then they argue and fight. I'm just like shut up with ya old asses. Break up or make up. I have three older brothers, an older sister, and two younger ones. Busy, busy, busy. I've had my heart broken twice and I don't know if I've ever broken any. I'm 15, five-feet-two inches, 115 pounds, and I naturally have super curly hair. But I straighten it because it's easier to manage. I wear an eight and one-half size shoe, and I'm a Northwest Coast hipster."

"Where in the Northwest?" He asked.

"Seattle"

"Damn." He said.

"DAMN...DAMN...DAMMMMN!" I snapped back.

"Babe?" He said in a questioning voice.

"Yes?" I equally replied.

"You're weird"

"Nahh…you're just normal."

"I'm far from normal."

"True"

"Yes, Ms. Little Feet…no big foot…kiss me?"

"No," I said.

"Why?"

"Because I want you to kiss me."

"Fine."

He got up and walked over to my side of the table and bends down and kisses me. His mouth was warm and gentle on mine, and it taste like strawberries. He gently bit my lip and I felt my body temperature heat up. I had to pull away before I jumped on this man. I pulled away and smiled at him. He looked at me, grinned, and said, "I knew you were gonna do that. I felt you gasp right after that too. You like it when I bite you, don't you?"

I laughed and said, "I'm not going to give you the satisfaction *My'trell*."

He made a puppy dog face and said: "Please Sekeya?"

"Okay I actually loved it; I pulled away because I didn't want to end up attacking you."

He smiled and bent down to kiss me again but not on my lips. He kissed me on my neck. bit me gently, and licked and sucked on me on the sky deck of the ship in the middle of the Atlantic Ocean.   He was crazy and I knew that I was going to attack him any second. I needed him to stop no matter how good it felt. I didn't want him to think I'm that kind of girl. So I reached behind him and I slapped his butt. Then he stood up and smiled at me again. "Why didn't you just tell me that you wanted me to stop? If I'm making you uncomfortable all you have to say is stop."

41

"I didn't want you to, but needed you to."

"Explain?" He said in a questioning voice.

"Okay, I really like you but I don't want you to think you can just f#@k me real good and leave me. I'm a virgin and I plan to stay that way; but we can cuddle, kiss, hug and stuff but besides that…nah."

"I didn't have that as my plan." He said. "I wanted to test your limits first. That's exactly what I wanted to hear girl! I'm tired of ratchets and I'm actually a virgin too. I've just had a few close calls but I always had something stopping me. It's kinda embarrassing though, and I don't tell very many people...so shhhh."

"Awe…well that's good."

"Yeah, but I wanna take you somewhere else now; can you dance little ma?"

"Yeah I guess. What kind of dancing?"

"Don't trip chocolate chip."

"Shut up yellow crayon."

"I'm going to let that slide but only because I like you."
He said.

And I replied to him. "You better."

I laughed and walked ahead of him and rushed to the
elevator to push the button.

"Stop now." I groaned and laughed as he tried to beat
me at pushing the button. "I can do it all by myself."

He smiled and tickled my sides saying, "you sure?"

I laugh as I tried to wiggle out of his arms, and I poked
the elevator's shiny silver button and smiled and said to
him: "See I got this."

"Yeah, I know," he said. "But I got you."

I smiled to him, stepped into the elevator, and said
softly said: "Whatever Bro."

PART III

FRESH

It was around 12:24 a.m. and we proceeded to the dance club downstairs. There we danced and hung out until two o'clock a.m. I got a little tired and he took me back to my personal room. I'm the only one in my room; my sister had her own room five doors down, and my parents had a master cabin.

When he noticed that I was the only one in my room and that I had two beds, he said: "If you want me to, I can just stay in your room so you're not lonely. I'll stay in the other bed."

I shrugged and said: "Okay, but don't try anything."

He smiled. "Okay I'll go and get my stuff out of my room. I hate the room with my brother, that man plays way too much.""That's exactly why I got my own."He looked at me and said as he started easing towards the door. "I should've got my own, and I'll be right back."

"Okay," I said.

About 10 minutes later he came back. I was about to take a shower so I was getting the bathroom situated; I got my soaps, shaving gel, lotion, facial scrub and oils for afterwards.

He knocked on the door and I let him in; I was in my bath robe. He smiled as I opened the door only to say: "You should wear more clothes around me, I might want to do something inappropriate to you."

I stepped to the side of the doorway and let him in and said; "I have underwear and a bra on. I'm not just going to get butt-naked and show you my goodies! But I'm going to take a shower now and I just wanted you to be in here so I wouldn't have to worry about having to get out just to let you in."He laughed and said: "Okay, but I'm going to take a shower too."

"I take long showers," I said, "so you can go first."

"You sure? I'll wait if you want me to."

"No it's fine, go ahead."

"Okay."

I set my iPod on my Dalking station, turned on my R&B playlist, and pulled a book out of my dresser. He was standing about twelve feet away from me; standing between the beds. He started bobbing his head to the music; removes his chain, earrings and watch and set it all on the counter next to my jewelry and purse. He looked at me and grinned. I looked back at him and shook my head. After twenty seconds he was standing right in front of me and he bent down and kissed me on the forehead. Then he took off his sleeveless jean jacket and shirt. I quickly noticed that he had a tattoo on his arm that read: "Man proposes, God disposes."

I look at his perfectly chiseled body and mumbled: "I thought you looked good with clothes on." He laughed and said, "I heard that...you know." But when he started to unbuckle his pants, I immediately looked up and said to him: "Umm you had better take your pants off somewhere else and get your penis out of my face. This is a big room, you have space."

47

He laughed and said, I'm sorry. I didn't mean to imply anything. I just like being close to you." He backed away, about five feet, and asked if this is okay now?" In which, I nodded my head and smiled. Then he bent over to take his shoes off. I noticed that there were no creases in his pants and his Nike socks matched too. That means he's organized and very particular and carries himself with respect. At least to me and I'm kind of weird like that. I notice everything in sight and don't forget anything, just like an elephant.

He pulled his pants down, then his super bright white basketball shorts. He was standing in front of me with a perfect body, a cocky smile, and I could feel him staring at me while I was trying not to look at him, even though over my book I snuck a few glances. He cleared his throat and I looked up, which was a mistake because his eyes we're glued on me and his long arms were open.

I laughed and said questioningly to him: "Yes, *My'trell*?"

"I need a hug." He said.

"Really?" I replied. "You're almost naked and yet you want to hug me."

He laughed and said to me: "You're almost naked too, if you take that robe off."

I could only respond by saying, "true." And I walked up to hug him and he cleared his throat again.

"Any problem?" He asked.

"Kind of." I said.

"What now, brat?" I laughed when he called me brat.

"Take off your robe then hug me."

"Why?"

"It's only fair, besides I saw you looking at me. And I know you liked what you saw."

"So what?" I said. "I don't hump every sexy, light skinned tatted guy I see."

Then he paused and grinned. "So you think I'm sexy?

And who said anything about humping."

I got ready to dispute it, but stopped myself and let him win. "Yes you're sexy."

I took off my robe, and did a slow 360 degree spin. His cockiness faded immediately, and his jaw drops "Um..Umm..Sekeya..Wow!"

"What?" I said.

"If you hug me wearing that I am going to end up having sex with you. But I want to wait until it's the right time. So before you get me excited you might want to put that robe on unless you want to."

I hugged him before he finished. "Aye...you're so sweet and considerate." I said.

His shoulders relaxed after I said that and he hugged me back and whispered in my ear: "I'm not going to be so considerate if you don't get me off of you girl. I'm ready to throw you on that bed and you don't want me to do that—right?"

"No." I lied, my mind said let him go but I couldn't.

Then he slowly released me. "I'm not going to let my male instinct take over," he said. "I really like you so I'm not going to let that happen to you."

I smiled and felt myself gravitating towards him. I walked so close to him that I could hear his heartbeat and I laid my head on his chest, but kept my hands behind my back. He wrapped his arms around me and I hugged him back. Then he bent down and touched my thighs. Next he picked me up and wrapped my legs around him. I held on tight and he kissed me on my neck, carried me to the bed, and set me down in the in the middle of it. He trailed kisses from my neck to my belly button. My pulse quickened and I started panicking and softly and calmly said to him; *"My'trell, we need to stop."*

"Why?" he said still kissing my torso.

I set up and told him; "I don't want to do this.""I'm sorry," he said. "I kind of got into a trance and started

51

thinking with that other head, if you know what I mean."

I giggled and told him. "How about you go get in the shower before something else happens?"

"Okay." He said, with a grin on his face.

And about twenty minutes later, *My'trell* yells from the shower, "Baby!" And I ignored him.

"Baby! Can you get my shorts I left them out there!?"

I, ignored him.

"I don't have a shirt either! And I already brushed my teeth and everything!"

Again, I ignored him.

"I know you heard me!" He shouted.

"I did, but I'm not getting up!" I shouted back. He walked out of the bathroom wet, glistening, butt naked and walked up to me and said "You're hella lazy."

I just looked him up and down, push him out of the way, and walked into the bathroom with my pajama shorts and tank top in hand.

I ran into the bathroom to take my shower and about 15 minutes later, I came out and he was dancing to some song by Chris Brown. He was basically dry humping the mattress and I started clapping my hands.

He turned around and stood there in his boxers. He smiled and started walking towards me. He hugged me, stepped back and yanked my towel off. I quickly covered myself, and ran into a corner so all he could see was my butt. He cleared his throat and laughed at me. I heard his footsteps coming closer. He got so close that I could hear his heart beat and feel his body heat on my back. He wrapped his arms around my waist and blew heavily on my neck. "I just wanted pay back," he said. Then he walked over to my bed and handed me my shorts and tank top that I set down when I walked out.

He kissed me on my cheek and said "I'll respect your boundaries," and I sat on my bed naked; not wanting to talk or show how nervous I was. And then he said to me, "just relax I'm not going to do anything bad."

I shrugged and replied, "Okay."

"I'm sorry." He said.

"It's fine. I mean I let you walk out naked."

"That's why I did it."

Then we both laughed and he told me, "Lie down and close your eyes."

"Hell no!" I snapped.

"I'm not going to violate you, just chill."

"What are you going to do?"

"Lie down and find out. But if you feel uncomfortable just sit up."

"Okay," I asked. "Is it sexual?"

"No, maybe sensual though."

"How?"

"You ask too many questions." He said.

"Fine."

I lay down, closed my eyes, and I felt a warm towel cover my body. My shoulders and above were the only thing showing. I felt another touch on my face; slowly from my forehead to my cheekbones and then to my neck. He did this very slowly and delicately like I was a baby or maybe his baby in his mind. He got to my neck and rubbed slowly in circles, just as delicately as he began. I felt him kiss my forehead, and I giggled. Then he kissed my neck and I said,"Don't or I'll get up."

"Okay, I'm sorry." He laughed.

The conversation suddenly ceased, and again we were quiet. He started drying my shoulders and when he was finished he was about to grab the towel and I said *"My 'trell"*.... But he laughed and said, "Give me a drop of trust?" I shrugged and said, "Okay don't f#@k up."

He then dried every single spot on my body with that warm towel. I was about to sit up but he kissed my shoulder and said "Not yet." So I lay back down and heard him open some type of lotion. He squirted some in his hands and rubbed it in his palms. Then he rubbed it on my shoulders and I immediately recognized the smell—it was my vanilla extract lotion that I put in the underwear section of my suit case. That *Nigga* was snooping through my stuff! But 'whatever' I thought; at that point all I was concerned with was the free full massage. It felt perfect and I guess I was a princess.

After he had moisturized my entire body he told me I could open my eyes then lifted my legs and slid my pink lace panties onto me and my black spandex shorts shortly after. Then he put one of his sweat shirts on me and took my hair out of its messy bun and put some of my coconut oil on it and ran his fingers through my hair. I felt so clean and relaxed.

'Thank you," I said in a calm and relaxed voice

He wrapped his arms around me and said "It was a pleasure little mama, your skin is so soft and delicate. You're just so…." His sentence trailed off.

"I'm so what?" I said.

"Small and Beautiful, like a diamond." He replied.

"Awwl...thank you sweet heart."

Then he smiled and kissed me. It was a passionate kiss—I wasn't expecting to feel all of the emotion that he was hiding in the kiss. We kissed for about five minutes straight and when I pulled away, I had a tear in my eye.

"Oh my god, what's wrong? Did I do something?" He asked in a worried tone.

"Yes you did something. I got all of the emotion that you put into that kiss."

"I know...so why are you crying?"

"Because..." For some reason, I couldn't explain.

But he insisted: "Explain baby girl."

"I'm going to miss you, when I go back home."

"I'm going to miss you more."

"You are going to text me?"

"Hell yeah," he abruptly replied. "Everyday until we see each other; Skype me, Oovoo, Facebook, and we can even write letters if you down with the old school style."

"Okay," I said, and another tear fell. Then *My'trell* kissed my tear, nose and lips.

"It's gonna be okay, save yourself for me and I'll do the same. I'll wait, that's what hands and lotion are for anyway."

Then we both laughed and I wiped my tears and said, "You're a fool."

"As long as I'm a fool for you, I'll be a fool until I die."

"You sure."

"Hell yeah...! There aren't any girls like you back home. If there are, they either are pretty with a horrible soul or a beautiful soul and an ugly face. You got both so I'm holding onto you as long as I can. I feel like since I have you now that I need you to stay. "

PART IV

FLIPPED

His eyes got glassy while he reclined back onto the headboard and shaking his head he mumbled, "What am I doing?"

"I don't know," I said. "You tell me what you're thinking and I'll figure it out."

"Well I'm 16 and you're 15, and I like you a lot Sekeya. I don't know why but I do. We've only known each other for almost two days now and I don't want to lose you already. You're like a young sage. Your eyes just tell stories but your mouth never utters a single word about what your eyes are feeling. I never thought about love at first sight, but I understand it now. You're just ...." He paused and closed his eyes.

"I'm just what?" I said in a soft tone. "You're just *flipped*. All the other girls I know are assholes and I'm not trying to be rude but they're just so simple and

61

irritating. I mean all of them except my sisters. But believe me, they too have their moments."

"Aww…thank you *My'trell*." Then I slid my body between his arms and rested my head on his chest. I started to speak again. "I think you feel like you like me more than you should and it's too good to be true huh? Like your imagination is playing a sick trick on you and you're awake, but the down fall is that you live in Detroit and I'm all the way in Seattle. You just want to stay forever on this beautiful boat in the middle of paradise, holding me in your arms, and never letting me go?"

Then he looked at me like I was crazy and he smiled, and then he said, "How did you know?"

"I followed your train of thought and I feel the same."

He exhaled and smiled again. "Thank you! He said. "I really didn't want to make this awkward; especially after the whole thing with me coming out naked and all, I thought it was a dead game."

"No, that was just plain comedy." I laughed.

"When I pulled your towel off I was about to go wild but I remembered that I have to respect you and all your wishes. I didn't want to make you afraid of me or to be upset with me."

Then I told him, "That's what I like about you."

"What about me?" He said.

"Your honesty."

"I like your everything."

"Thank you *My-My*."

"You're welcome gorgeous."

"Want to play a game?"

"What game?" He asked.

"Questions or Truth or Dare?"

"Questions? If we play truth or dare we might end up doing something inappropriate."

"Okay, you start."

"Would you date me, even with the distance?"

"Yes, *My'trell*. If I want to date you, I'm sure we could work around that."

"Good, my turn." He said.

"Have you ever felt this way *My-My?*"

"No, and I never thought I would." He pulled me tighter into his arms and kissed my forehead.

We talked all night until we saw the sunrise and we went out onto my balcony and watched the sky change colors. For the next six days, we talked, swam, shopped, kissed, slept and cuddled for the rest of the entire cruise. The last day we had together, we stood in the lobby of the ship holding hands and kissing as our families tried to pull us away. We kissed one final time and a single tear fell from each of our eyes. We hugged and wiped each others tears away. He pulled me tight and said "I love you, it won't be long until we see each other again Sekeya."

"I love you too and don't forget to text me tonight?"

"I will never forget." He said.

"Bye *My-My*."

"Bye KeKe."

Our families pulled us away and we made it to the car. I finally turned on my cell phone only to be receiving a text from *My'trell* instantly. It was a picture of us kissing that we took on his iPhone. I saved the picture to my Android phone. Seconds later I got a text from him saying, "I miss you already. Girl you got me *flipped*. Listen to a song called *'Best thing in My life' by Chris Brown.*"

I smiled and put my headphone plugs in each ear and played the song he requested. Just as I love him, I love that song. But most of all, I got *My-My flipped*.

To Be Continued….

 Yazmine Mobley is a young girl that lives in the Central District neighborhood in Seattle. She has four siblings and is the nerd of the family. She is fourteen years old and lives in a world of controversy that she struggles to fight her way through. She is a 9th grade student with all the up's and down's that you'd expect from a teenager. With her sassy smile and the silly moments that she has had, she is still an all around good kid!

About Young Urban Authors

Young Urban Authors has a mission to empower young adults by equipping them with the necessary tools that can lead to rewarding careers as entrepreneurs, through appreciation of the literary arts and the knowledge of available opportunities to publish their own literary work. At-risk youth are targeted for program recruitment, such as delinquents, dropouts, pregnant teens, etc; however, the program is also open to non at-risk youth. The purpose is to collectively empower residential youth seeking sustainable skills and careers that the publishing arts have to offer.

Here is Your Chance to Support a Great Youth Organization!

The Young Urban Authors Project is thrilled to announce that ten of the youth in our program have become published authors. These young people currently have books selling on our website as well as large online book retailers. We are so proud of their accomplishments, and want to continue providing this same opportunity to other youth in the community.

Word of our program has spread throughout the community. We now have a waiting list of young people who would like to take part in the program during the winter and spring quarter. In order to continue our mission, and make this a reality for those youth, we really need your help.

Our goal is to serve 20 youth per year. Some of these young people would not have an opportunity to achieve this on their own, nor would they have the tools to do so. The average cost for one young person in the program is $1,000.00.

Please help us reach our goal of serving 20 young people per year. Your donation is tax deductible, and we appreciate whatever you can give. Know that you are helping to empower our youth and provide a brighter future in today's world. We partnered with the Seattle Neighborhood Group in our efforts to (develop) and expand our program, providing more youth with a chance to be heard.

Checks should be made payable to, "Young Urban Authors". If you prefer to donate online, please go to our website: www.youngurbanauthors.org.

There is no better feeling then knowing you have helped a child. If you have any questions, suggestions, or comments about the Young Urban Author Project, please contact us. My contact information, as well as that of the Seattle Neighborhood Group, is provided below.

Frankie Roe,

c/o Young Urban Authors

1810 E. Yesler

Seattle, WA 98122

Seattle Youth Violence Prevention Initiative

The Seattle Youth Violence Prevention Initiative (SYVPI) tackles the issue of youth violence with an approach that incorporates evidenced-based strategies along with home-grown, youth-and community-created programs. The goals of the Initiative are to achieve a 50% reduction in juvenile court referrals for violence and a 50% reduction in suspensions and expulsions from selected middle schools due to violence-related incidents.

The Initiative funds some of these home-grown programs through Community Matching Grants. These programs supplement existing Initiative services by providing positive, healthy activities that support a safe, non-violent lifestyle. The Young Urban Authors' Project is one of the first grantees under the Community Matching Grant program. It helps to fulfill the mission of the Initiative by assisting our youth to find and share their voices through the written word.

Other YUA Titles

Found – Journey to Salvation by Tayonna Gault

Standing Alone – A collection of mini stories by Mattie Alexander

A letter to my Grandma by Kylea Spears

Stuck in this World Alone by Alrick Hollingsworth

Young Life – Hanan Soulaiman

Leading Thru Change – Standing Above the Crowd by Amina Mohammed

Long Way Down by Tajh'Nique Richardson

My Cry Out – The Story of My Tears by April Wilburn

Blasian Drive – Having the Determination to Continue by Shalena Duong

Life As It Is by Jennifer Gutierrez

The Journey of a Solid Soldier by Jimmy Phin

Hi Drama – A Collection of Short Stories by Karlina Khorn

A Walk Down Memory Lane by Monique Blockman

Wrote This Because of You by CurDesia' Hudson